# A Big Spider

Written by Jo Windsor

Rigby

In this book
you will see
a big spider.

tarantula

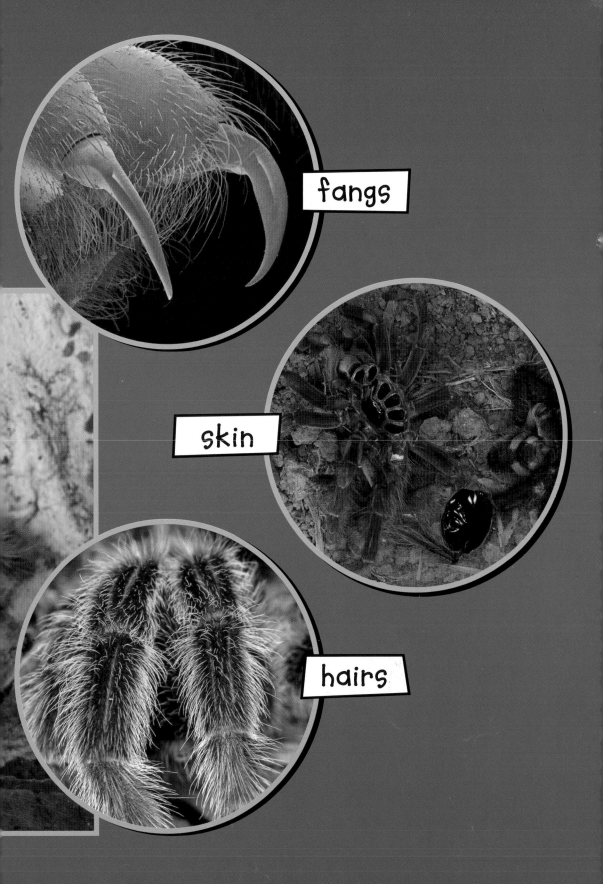

fangs

skin

hairs

3

Look at this spider!

It is the biggest spider in the world.

This spider lives in the forest.

This spider lives...

in a tree  Yes? No?

in a burrow Yes? No?

4

tarantula

The spider has lots of hairs.

It has hairs on its legs.
It has hairs on its head.
It has hairs on its body.

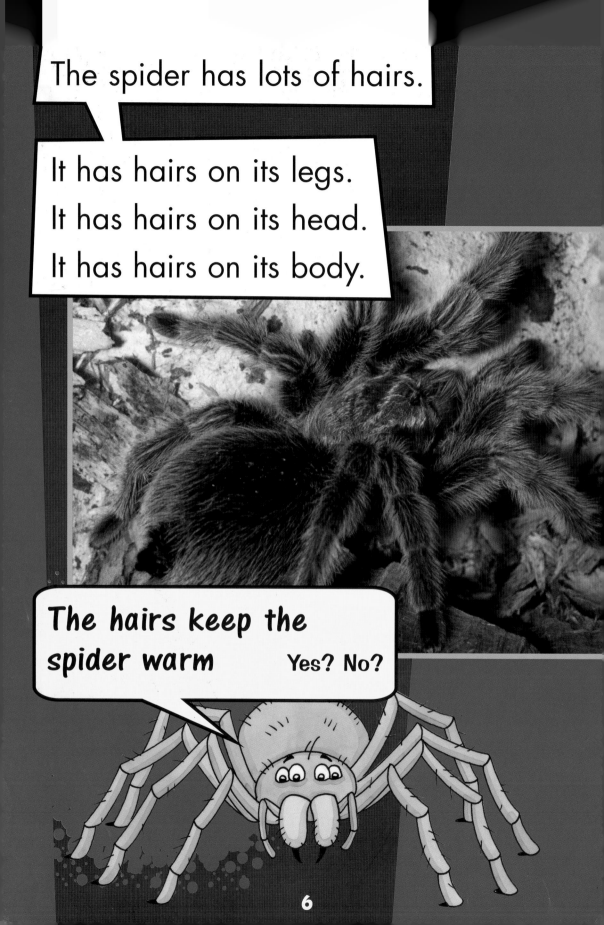

The hairs keep the spider warm     Yes? No?

The hairs can come out.

The hairs can sting you.

# Look at the spider's fangs!

The spider has big fangs.
Look out!

The spider...

digs with its
fangs                    Yes? No?

gets food with
its fangs                Yes? No?

The spider shows its big fangs.

The spider's fangs say, "Go away!"

The big spider likes to eat.
It gets food with its fangs.
It catches its food
in its big fangs.

The spider eats...

birds    Yes? No?

grass    Yes? No?

frogs    Yes? No?

The spider lives
under the ground.
The spider lives in a burrow.

It lives in a burrow
that was made by a rat.

The rat lives with the
spider          Yes? No?

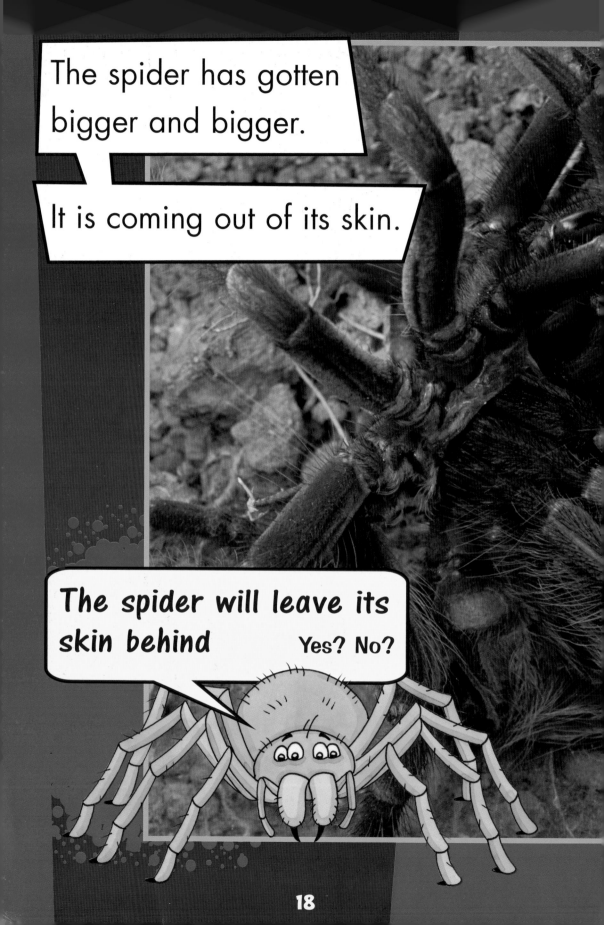

The spider has gotten bigger and bigger.

It is coming out of its skin.

The spider will leave its skin behind        Yes? No?

Look at the spider!

The big spider has
a new skin!

# Index

# Labels

Look at the spider!

# Which labels will you use?

hairs

fangs

foot

skin

eyes

hand

head

ear

body

legs

# Word Bank

burrow

fangs

forest

legs